CHERRY MOON

LITTLE POEMS BIG IDEAS
MINDFUL OF NATURE

DEDICATION

Victoria, Gideon, Thatcher, Jacquelyn,
Joseph, Fiona, Arlo and Gareth

Published by ZaZaKids Books
in association with
Troika Books
First published 2019

1 3 5 7 9 10 8 6 4 2

Text copyright © Zaro Weil 2019
Illustrations copyright © Junli Song 2019
The moral rights of the author and illustrator have been asserted
All rights reserved
A CIP catalogue record for this book is available from the British Library

ISBN 978-1-909991-94-1

Printed in Poland

Designed by Sarah Pyke

ZazaKids Books
www.zazakidsbooks.com

Troika Books Ltd.
Well House, Green Lane, Ardleigh CO7 7PD, UK
www.troikabooks.com

CHERRY MOON

LITTLE POEMS BIG IDEAS
MINDFUL OF NATURE

ZARO WEIL
ILLUSTRATED BY JUNLI SONG

morning

I want to be
where wild things are
and be part of
well

everything

ACKNOWLEDGMENTS

One day when I was little, I went for a walk with my father in the woods.
It was May. Sunset. Looking up, the sky slid into pink wisps as the woods turned
a strange, incandescent green. Some birds took off, shaking the leaves as they
flew away. A squirrel raced up one of the trees. The full moon now looked almost red.
Like a distant ripe cherry.

I took my father's hand because nothing had ever felt so perfect to me.
So mysterious. Or powerful.

I never forgot that twilight in the woods; that pink and green sunset,
the flying birds, the racing squirrel and that cherry moon.

These pictures stayed with me, as vivid as ever, until they conspired to persuade
me to recreate that electrifying sense of oneness with nature I had experienced
all those years ago. And that is how I came to write Cherry Moon.

Another inspiration was seeing the magical artwork of Junli Song for the first time.

Another was and is the continued support of dear friend and long time editor,
the savvy Judith Elliott, along with wonderful colleagues;
Roy Johnson, Martin West, Jo Hardacre, and Sarah Pyke. And how
luckily for me, my poet muse and inspiration, Jane O Wayne.

And to readers out there who dare to dream big, think wild and long to experience
nature in new and mysterious ways, it is for you I have written this book.

Contents

Listen earth   10

Snoring dog   12

Giddy with dawn   13

Plum tree (spring)   15

Snapping turtle's haiku   19

After the purple rains   20

How does the flower open   24

Tip-top of the world   26

Red red red   28

Dogwood flower   32

Pipsqueak   32

Strawberry   33

Bluebells   33

Such luck   35

Just-born bugs   36

Little jellybean toe shoes   36

Gosling's haiku   37

Hippo's haiku   37

River's haiku   38

River's song   39

Life is big   42

The linden tree is out   44

Wonderfulness   46

I spot them   48

Daytime   50

Be quiet sun   50

Shiny sun   50

Hum and buzz   51

A parade of beast-doodles   52

You and the stars   56

Moon things   56

Thorny branches   56

Worm's haiku   57

Cherry moon   59

Flicker and flash   60

Waterfall's song   64

Small green frog's haiku   66

Ladybird's song   67

This tiny bean   68

Dappling sun   72

Plum tree (summer)   74

Wild as the wind   78

Bats   81

Me without myself   82

Ten ways to catch the moon   84

Song of being together   87

Elephant tusks   88

When I heard the nightingale   93

Song of summer   94

Flash   96

Tell me a story   98

This great old tree   100

Between the cracks   104

How does the stone smell   105

Plum tree (autumn)   106

Wilderness howls   110

Tiny tiny bird   112

Mountain's song   114

Wind's song   114

Time's song   115

Every little pebble's song   115

Mixumgatherum   117

How to get lost   118

The leaves were a-shake   122

Don't be bored rock   124

This way and that   127

Mudpuddling tonight   128
When the beast   131
Fat moon   133
Hide and seek   134
Plum tree (winter)   137
Fairy lights   140
Silence   141
If all clouds were earth   142
Polar bear's haiku   145
Duskingtide   148
All tangled up   150
This day is too big   150
Thank you tree   151
Poor snail   153
Letter to the moon   154
Stop the world   156
Flea's haiku   158
Whale's haiku   158
Rain's haiku   159
Noisy toe's haiku   159
Story time orchestra   161
A confetti sky   162
Afternoon showers   162
Morning's haiku   163
Twilight's haiku   163
Perfect crystal's haiku   164
Snowy owl's haiku   164
Snow's song   165
Such luck again   166
Winter sun's haiku   167
Crunchandslide   169
Preposterous penguins   171
Trees and me   175

LISTEN EARTH

listen earth

make sure
your buried rainbows
come up today
just like last spring

and a million springs
before that

11

SNORING DOG

can you hear that sound?
that's my dog snoring
he wakes up the stars
who wake up the moon
who wakes up the sea
who wakes up the earth
who wakes up the trees
who wake up the birds
who wake up

me!

GIDDY WITH DAWN

not even light and
the birds are
giddy with dawn
every one a-warbling from
slate-shadowed branches
every one a-winging through
just waking leaves
every one a-roistering under
a velveteen soft
up-rising sun

PLUM TREE (spring)

rollicking pink puffs
tremble under
woolly March clouds
wind's blowing hard

hang on blossoms

birds and I
grow ripe with worry

Past

18

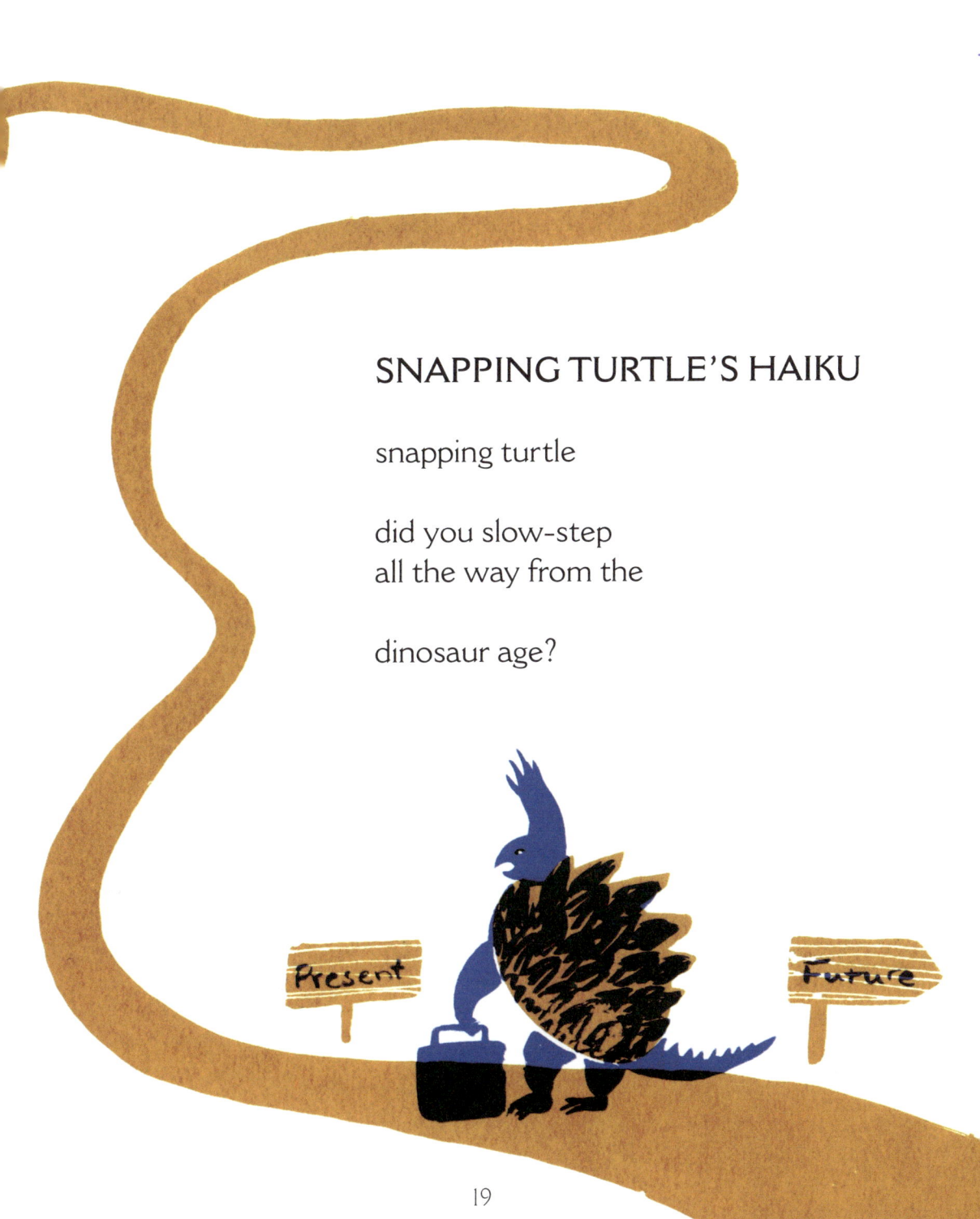

SNAPPING TURTLE'S HAIKU

snapping turtle

did you slow-step
all the way from the

dinosaur age?

AFTER THE PURPLE RAINS

after the purple rains

restless clouds of

crayon-box wildflowers

hurtle and tumble

skimble-skamble

harum-scarum

helter-skelter

in between rock beds

over squelchy slopes

through stone walls

to up-pop

outside my window

how very luck-dazzle

how very spring

HOW DOES THE FLOWER OPEN?

Q   how does the flower open
A   in petal time

Q   how does the rain fall
A   in drop time

Q   how does the bird fly
A   in wing time

Q   how does the sea roll
A   in wave time

Q   how does the dog talk
A   in bark time

Q how does the tree grow
A in root time

Q how does the cloud form
A in puff time

Q how do the planets travel
A in star time

Q how does the earth turn
A in all the time

TIP-TOP OF THE WORLD

such a quiet sky

can't hear you at all today
not even one note of blue
for this afternoon
fine fine water
floats down from the
tip-top of the world
soft-spreading a silent song
a thick grey cloud over
everything

such a quiet sky

with only
a festival of frogs
singing here
leaping there
catching the delicious mist
on their long tongues

RED RED RED

each year I'm waiting

for the cherries to ripen

each year I'm waiting

for the birds to eat them all

each year I'm waiting

to get there first

chirp chirp chirp

laugh the fat-bellied birds

merrily hopping over

last night's sticky sweet

red red red carpet of

beautifully pecked pits

DOGWOOD FLOWER

this dogwood flower and I met yesterday
we were both very pleased
and spent a long time
thanking one another
for summoning
such a scrumptious
sunny afternoon

PIPSQUEAK

. . . and have we discussed
the pipsqueak blossoms
on minuscule stems
buried in tiny
grass spears?

STRAWBERRY

if I were as red as you
as sweet
as round
I'd wind up in a basket too

BLUEBELLS

sprung from blue sky
fed by green rain
pushing always
towards April

and me

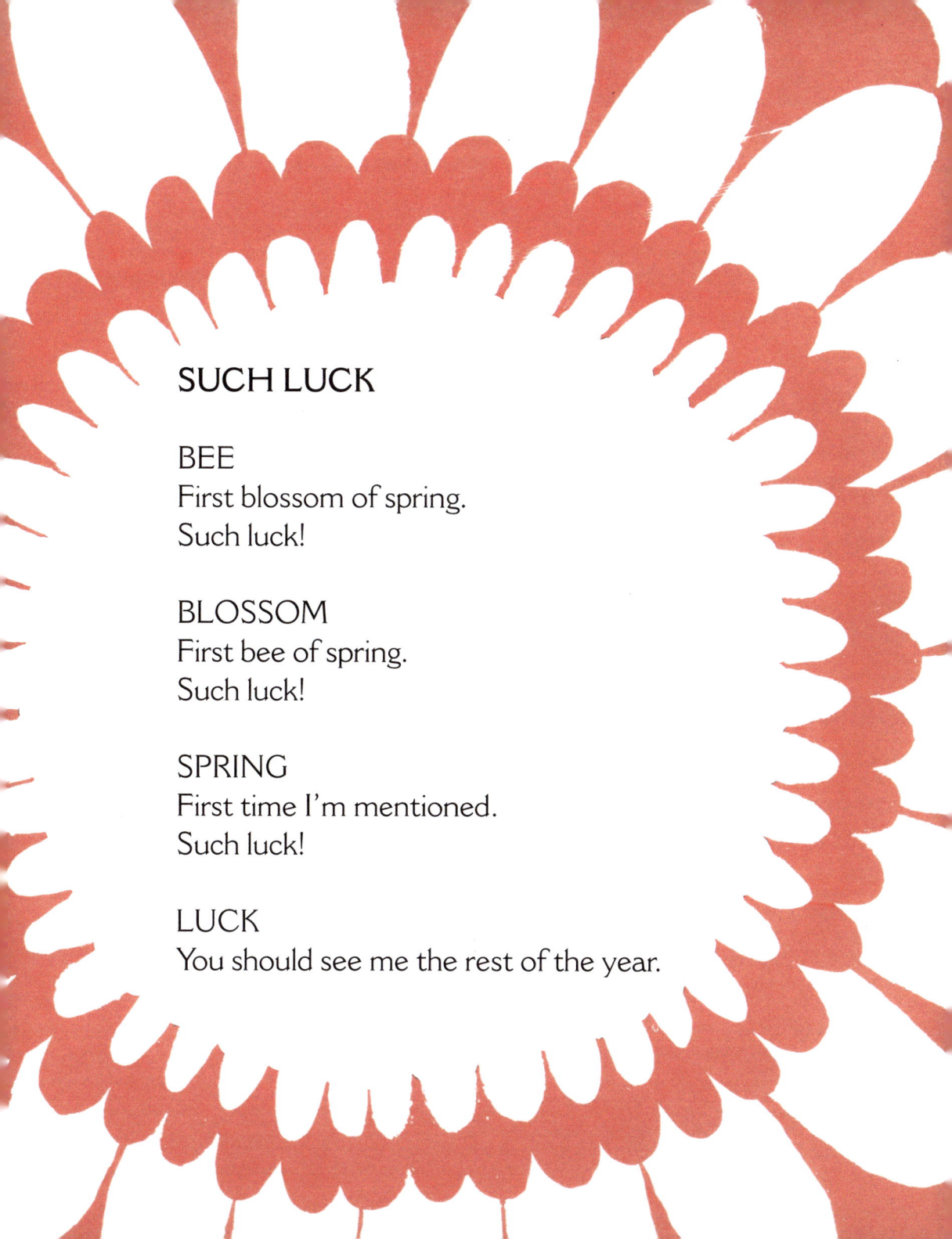

SUCH LUCK

BEE
First blossom of spring.
Such luck!

BLOSSOM
First bee of spring.
Such luck!

SPRING
First time I'm mentioned.
Such luck!

LUCK
You should see me the rest of the year.

JUST-BORN BUGS

wriggles of
tiny shadows in the dirty pond
inky live threads flitting by

look!

just-born bugs
and already
etching out their first spring

LITTLE JELLYBEAN
TOE SHOES

this kitten wears
little jellybean toe shoes
underneath her paws
so when she jumps
she leaps
so high

so sweet

GOSLING'S HAIKU

good golly
giggled the gaggle
of googly-eyed goslings

seen mama?

HIPPO'S HAIKU

think slow
take my time
squish my toes
in muddy water

dig my fine shine

RIVER'S HAIKU

you'd never guess

but it's taken forever

learning to roll

so well

RIVER'S SONG

everyone
and I mean everyone
has something to say
to the river
some nod their heads and
take their time
others wave their arms or
race by talking
while some just listen

to what the river has to say

LIFE IS BIG

life is big
thought the grasshopper
landing in
green folds
between
grass blades

life is big
thought the snake
slithering fat coils
along the
rusty fence

life is big
thought the beetle
scuttling over the
rustling
aspen leaf

life is big
thought the caterpillar
squeezing inside a
fresh cabbage

life is big
thought the ant
carrying the
apple seed
to its
nest

life is big
thought the mouse
zigzagging between
sugar-scented
weeds

life is big
thought the cat
staring hard
at the blue sky of
diving birds

life is big
thought the dog
chasing round
trees loud with
scampering
squirrels

life is big
thought the fly
circling a
thousand and one
times
round my head

life is big
I thought
seeing the
whole wide world
while walking home
real slow

THE LINDEN TREE IS OUT

the linden tree is out!
the linden tree is out!
cry the hungry new flutterbugs
as they anxiously follow
sweetened trails
loop through
dew-speckled air
fly breathless in and out of a
tender-leafed canopy
all the way to a

single beckoning linden flower

they can finally call home

WONDERFULNESS

there it is

opening in a burst
of honeyed sundrops
right before my eyes

that rarest of rare plants
a bee orchid

looking just like a delicate yellow-black bee
sucking a fragile yellow-purple-black orchid

but instead of stopping
breathless to

admire its wonderfulness and
springfulness

I walk right on by

my head still in a fuzzy
winter-clumsy cloud of
must-dos and don't-forgets

I SPOT THEM

I spot them
just outside the gate
fields of bright red poppies
flinging themselves carelessly
with every shift of wind song

towards light and morning

49

DAYTIME

sun slow-soars
towards morning
night cracks open
light seeds scatter

everywhere

BE QUIET SUN

be quiet sun!

frog is having a daydream
naturally he dreams of night
and a million moon songs

SHINY SUN

shiny sun
so bright
so tiny
I could pick you up
and hold you
in my hand forever

I even heard
some people call you

buttercup

HUM AND BUZZ

when the world is so yellow
the air so full of
hum and buzz
I just close my eyes
and breathe in big
and then

one more time

A PARADE OF
BEAST-DOODLES

when I opened up today
and unwrapped the morning
I found a present

a sky full of clouds
all puff-pomps and shine-streaks
bubble-whites and lace-feathers
a canopy of stipple-shapes

a parade of beast-doodles and
all I could do was
lie down
to skybig
to clouddream
and wonder
what I might unwrap

this afternoon

54

55

YOU AND THE STARS

mud puddle
mud puddle
it seems such a long way
between you and the stars
but sometimes
I just want to roll
in you both

MOON THINGS

water swells
each day it
chases the shoreline
till
sea things
moon things
call it back

THORNY BRANCHES

pale quince blossoms
on thorny branches
thin fingers reaching out
to grab March
by the scruff

WORM'S HAIKU

in and out of earth
magic worms
excavating
tiny roads
expressly
for April

CHERRY MOON

cherry moon
smooth
red
so perfectly shined
were you ever really

a blossom

FLICKER AND FLASH

so many dragonflies

translucent whirligigs
each a tailspin
of flicker and flash
under this
perfumed peach sky

a thousand
tinselly rainbows
glance off wings
a million
miniature wind-curls
dance round them all

such capricious
summer sprites

cavorting forwards
hovering backwards

as though they have
all the time in the world
as though summer

will never end

WATERFALL'S SONG

born in some long-ago
    flicker of time
water arrives
    first
a fragile drop
a quiet trickle till
    another time-tremble
    sends it braiding through earth
surging all the way to
    today

                    sheer-bubbling
                    fast-flowing
                    rock-rolling down cliffs
                    a ceaseless torrent plunging
                    into perpetual swirls
                        dangerous dark pools

                    and all the while
                    crystalline spray wildly
                      laces through air
                    a bonanza of rainbow flecks
                    sparkling with abandon

the wind is enchanted

hurriedly flies off
    (colourful new mist in tow)
vanishing in a breath from
today

only to be found
slow-seeping into
    long-ago legends
 or trickling quietly

    into the future

SMALL GREEN FROG'S HAIKU

small green frog
hops onto the ridge
of the sticky jampot
of course
he's invited to tea

LADYBIRD'S SONG

yoohoo!
good morning!

have you seen
my new polka dots this season?
so perfect
each dot so
very very perfect!

what?

no?

OK
I'll tiptoe a little closer

wait!

don't be scared
I only eat
very very tiny things

THIS TINY BEAN

this tiny bean
was sprung from a bean flower
and fed by the sun
blue and yellow birds
sought it out
weightless butterflies
rested on its quivering petals
generations of insects
climbed up and down its
perfectly formed pod
rainbow water
splashed its roots

clearly
this tiny bean
was never in a million years
just any old
bean

DAPPLING SUN

dappling sun

                        bounces in dots

over petals and grass

                        jumps in sprinkles

from tree to tree

                        hops in flecks

all over the sidewalk

leaps in freckles

round puddles and walls

so many speckles

so many spots

so many skips

so much summer

PLUM TREE (summer)

here at last
here at last
purple dripping like honey
down my chin

winter?
never heard of it

WILD AS THE WIND

if I were wild as the wind
I'd cannonball around the world

        atop a whizzing zigzaggery
        night-streaking through
        star spangles

    swaggering through sun whorls

      untameable
          unstoppable
              uncatchable

if I were wild as the wind
I'd somersault all the way to
that dangerous terrible edge

      of far away
      where I'd gather my forces

              tempestuous
                    tumultuous
                          turbulent

      and start again

BATS

almost midnight

bats dart
like phantom jets
round my head

really

can't they tell

I'm nothing like a bug

ME WITHOUT MYSELF

the sun has run away

spinning out of control
till in a sizzling flare of
electric yellow it
streaks towards earth
plunging headlong

right into my street

suddenly trapped
in the blinding glare
nothing dares move or
even breathe

summer-hot colours
dissolve as
shadows peel off like
cling film

everything now laid
flat
white
and no creature venturing out
in search of cool or dark
has a clue that they are
missing a detail of themselves

their shadow

even my shadow
splits without a word
leaving me suspended

me without myself

so
I wait under a tree
like every other half-shape   for things shadowy to return
for twilight   cautiously
for the sun to come back   moon in tow
and tumble   rounding out the world till
like it always does   nothing is missing
behind the city

                                   where we are all
                                   reunited at last with those
                                   moody tangles
                                   deep folds
                                   mythic twists

                                   of darkness

TEN WAYS TO CATCH THE MOON

1 put it carefully into a jar of stars

2 paste it to your bedroom ceiling with strong shadows

3 wrap it with beams you borrowed from the sun earlier

4 save it in a special drawer next to your little silver comets

5 cast your fishing line very very far

6 climb a ladder to the top of everything

7 drop it in the water till it bounces over to you

8 ask the man who lives up there to throw it down to you

9 climb a tree and untangle it gently from the leaves

10 jump up and down till it loses balance and topples out of the sky

SONG OF BEING TOGETHER

when the river is together with its ripples
    it's one
when the grass is together with its green
       it's one
when the mountain is together with its peak
        it's one
when the moon is together with its shine
         it's one
when the tree is together with its leaves
          it's one
when the flower is together with its scent
           it's one
when the rain is together with its drops
            it's one
when the butterfly is together with its colours
             it's one
when I sing and dance and make up stories
              I'm one

ELEPHANT TUSKS

these long smooth tusks
are mine
passed down to me by
my family
who are older than your family
it would be very bad luck
for you humans
to take my tusks
you don't need them
besides
it is clearly my ancient
elephant right
to keep them

WHEN I HEARD
THE NIGHTINGALE

when I heard the nightingale
it was so beautiful
I fastened my words
to the music

SONG OF SUMMER

giddily fat
slickly black
bugs
dazzled by sun-shimmer
fevered by heat-sting
rush on ungainly legs along scorched earth
squeezing themselves into some small
hollow of
some tree somewhere while
tiny hovering things
finding the sky too thin for flight
give up
head for a million dark spots
lilliputian places hidden beneath
in between and behind other places
to wait it out

till only the crickets
cunningly dotted on
branch leaf and stem
rub their legs together
as fast as they can in a
grinding
tuneless
completely reassuring

song of summer

FLASH

flash

just spotted the
brightest red
in the world the
glowingest orange
in the universe the
hottest blue
in the cosmos
all
on one
small bird
it was so bright
I had to look away

but the bird just smiled

and took off

a flutter of razz-dazzle
soaring towards some new
tangerine-twizzle
of a galaxy

TELL ME A STORY

tell me a story
tell me now or
I will wait here
till earth sea moon and stars
all talk

all at once

THIS GREAT OLD TREE

this great old tree dreams
with its tangling hungry roots
daily pushing their way through
billion-year earth to
ancient buried water

this great old tree dreams
with its voluminous trunk
daily rounding and circling
slow ring by slow ring
growing century by century

this great old tree dreams
with its twisting branches
thrusting here turning there
daily seeking strands of
quicksilver light

this great old tree dreams
with its fragile veined leaves
trembling to every fresh
wind wave
daily searching sequinned
sky drops of water

this great old tree dreams
with its rope-knotted bark
daily giving shelter
to a universe of small creatures
who call it home

this great old tree dreams
with its boughs of fruit which
daily fall into the mouths of
beasts and birds
who grow fat from
such sweet food

this great old tree dreams
with its infinite summer shade
when I stop to
daily rest under its dappled arbour
to dream all the dreams
I can possibly dream

BETWEEN THE CRACKS

last night hides
between the cracks
starry night rolls in
under the door
yesterday's pale moon stretches
through my bedroom window
a galaxy of dust whirls
around my pillow
sunrise shadows
rustle the quiet

I wonder what's going to slip in next
through the very same cracks

HOW DOES THE STONE SMELL

how does the stone smell
how does the grass sound
how does the tree fly

however I say

how does the day roll
how does the moon spin
how does the cloud sing

however they feel

how does the cricket read
how does the lion think
how does the walrus talk

the way they always have

PLUM TREE (autumn)

plums
hope you're inside that branch
can't see a thing
but if I run up close
and open my ears

sap roars
like tree lions

WILDERNESS HOWLS

wilderness howls

when wind
carries the scent of
wildflower blaze

when trails of birds
thread gaudy air ribbons
between tree tangle

when water up-bubbles
to varnish earth in clear gleam
(rainbows where you'd least expect them)

when silky-shined rocks reveal lost paths
going dangerous spiky directions

when candy-coloured bugs feast inside
tiny leaf glints of sun shadow

it's all true
the world re-enchants

when wilderness howls

TINY TINY BIRD

sundown

tiny tiny bird
perches on top of the pine cone
watches my fading shadow
follows its every move and when
she flies off into sky blush
through a shake and shimmy of
dusk green needles
my shadow and I miss her
long to catch up

think it would be fun to
shake and shimmy our way as well
all the deep night
all the deep way to

sun-up

MOUNTAIN'S SONG

even if you can't see
over my peak
don't worry
I'll tell you a story later
about the other side

WIND'S SONG

so why wait?
come on
keep up
I'll get behind you

hey!
just helping

TIME'S SONG

on and
on and
on and
on
not ahead
not behind
stopping only for a
dream or two

EVERY LITTLE
PEBBLE'S SONG

I celebrate ancient earth
I salute ancient wind
I congratulate ancient waters

they made me who I am today

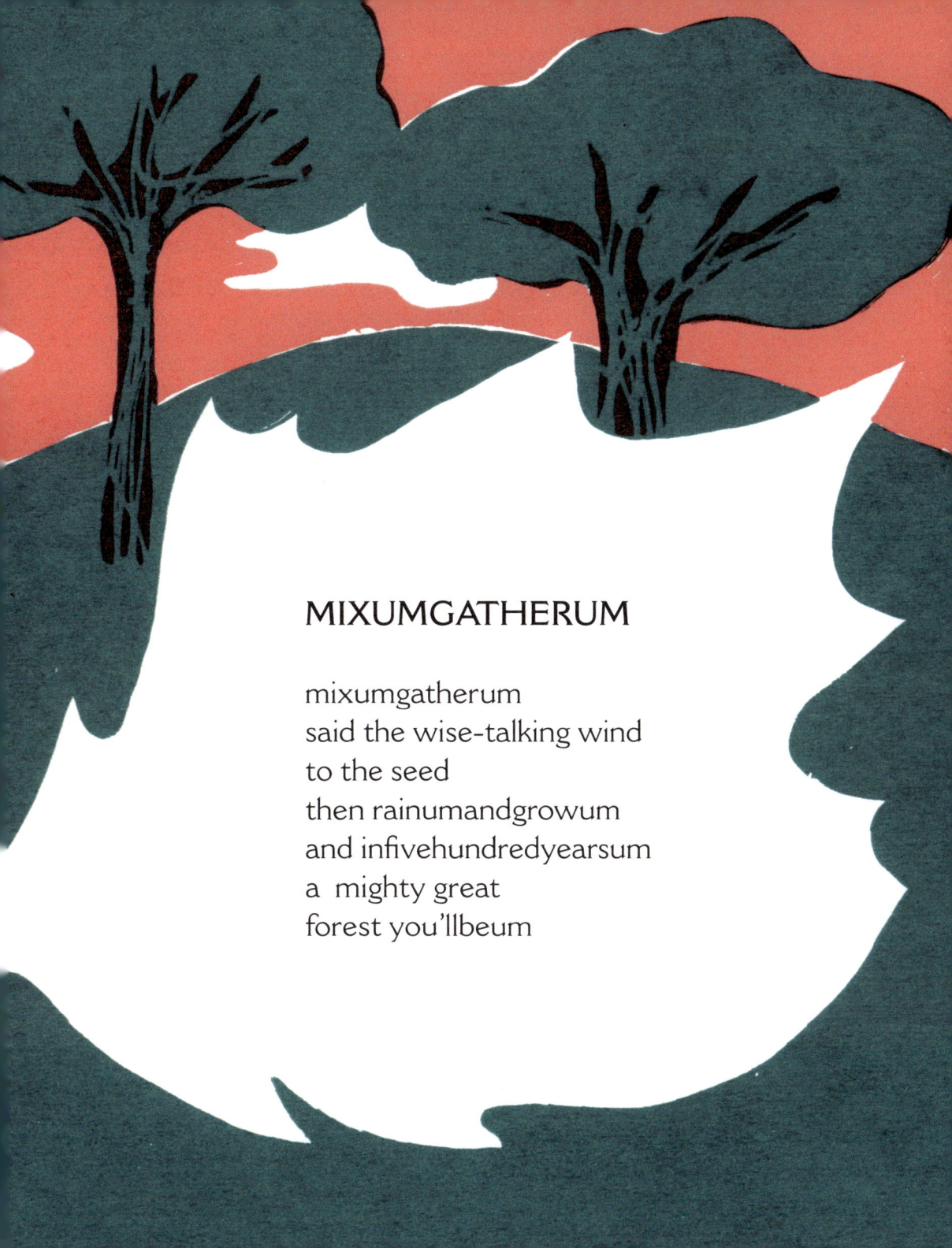

MIXUMGATHERUM

mixumgatherum
said the wise-talking wind
to the seed
then rainumandgrowum
and infivehundredyearsum
a mighty great
forest you'llbeum

HOW TO GET LOST

ask your shoes to walk you over the edge of the map
   or
fly off with your biggest fattest birthday balloon
   or
dive into the notes of your favourite song
   or
explore a hidden cave of stirring stories
   or
hitch a ride on anything exploring anywhere
   or
run your fingers over the globe till they can't remember
where they started

or

trade places with a time traveller

or

dress up as a falling leaf and see where you land

or

join an ant colony and journey to underground kingdoms

or

hold on tight to the north wind

or

travel quietly into the deepest forest you can find . . .

or

or

or

or

or . . .

THE LEAVES
WERE A-SHAKE

the leaves were a-shake
they had heard the news
birds passed it on
moss spread the word
faded sunflowers told everyone
ivy twined it round
ducks splashed it out loud
spiders spun the story
ants mentioned it over and over
in passing
for everyone knew
tomorrow
autumn would be heading their way

naturally
the leaves got the picture and
overnight curled
yellowed and oranged
next
they signalled a crinkly wind-call
to each other
whispering in a thousand
thin rustles

time to take off
time to take off

DON'T BE BORED ROCK

don't be bored rock
once you were orange fire
thundering down some
mountain slope or
hurtling silver sleek
through deep sky

maybe you were thrown up
sputtering red by
an ancient fuming volcano or
born with the planet in a
starless galactic bang

to be carved sharp by ice
rounded by raging wind

but whichever it was
being still now is good
after all

you have so much to remember

THIS WAY AND THAT

the hills roll this way and that
covered in trees swaying this way and that
filled with leaves swirling this way and that
surrounded by birds flying this way and that
all adrift in the wind soaring this way and that
everyone knowing winter won't wait

MUDPUDDLING TONIGHT

mudpuddling tonight
sloshgurgling
all the way home through
a well-shined slipstream of
a million and one raindrops
lit by
a million and one moondots

WHEN THE BEAST

when the beast
swaggers and stomps
round my bed at night
it doesn't bother me
lemon drop stars
and a mango moon
are just outside

FAT MOON

fat moon
please don't fall
through the sky
it's ok
you'll be a sliver soon

HIDE AND SEEK

I decided to play a game with quiet

hide and seek
my turn
I slipped into the woods
looking for quiet
instead
a cacophony of forest-crackle
a hullabaloo of beast-babble
sprang towards me while
a tweedledum of pandemonium
circled above
it was a free-for-all
and even the sun
jangled copper
between the leaves

so much for the forest

I went to the sea
searching for quiet
but the waves trumpeted
a rumbling ruckus
a crash of crinkle-crests while

squarking gulls sky-dived into
wind-trembled sea and
seashells crunched underfoot
as a medley of
fat green seaweed
slapped the sand
non-stop non-stop

so much for the sea

but then I turned
and quiet tagged me
I stopped
forest stopped
sea stopped

I found quiet
it must have been hiding
the whole time
inside my words
inside of me

PLUM TREE (winter)

you may not look like much now
however
if I stand under your branches
and wait a little while
juicy things will fall into my mouth
like sweet snow

FAIRY LIGHTS

fairy lights
after the storm
gossamer cloud drops
quiver under still
damp stars

SILENCE

silence waits
inside and out
and like my poem
takes its time

I have to be ready
to hear it

IF ALL CLOUDS WERE EARTH

if all clouds were earth
and all earth were skies
and all skies were suns
and all suns were stars
and all stars were rivers
and all rivers were rocks
and all rocks were fish
and all fish were mountains
and all mountains were birds
and all birds were trees
and all trees were people
and all people were flowers
then if I picked one flower

I'd hold absolutely everything
in my hand

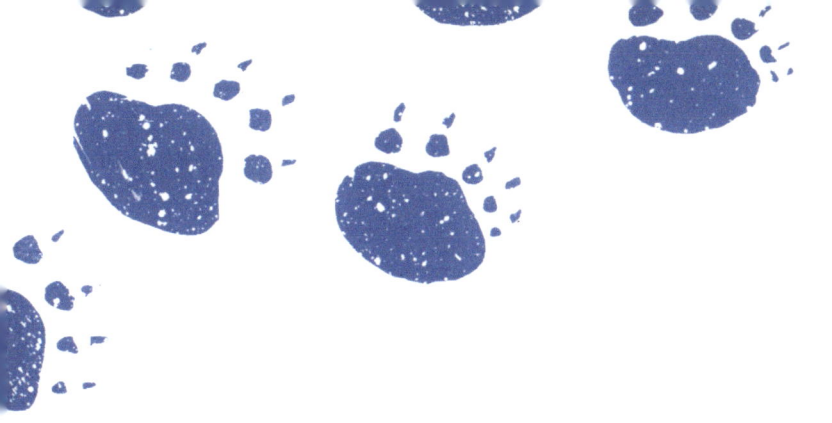

POLAR BEAR'S HAIKU

belly blank as snow
ache walks with each step
as hope melts
and fear drips
like ice

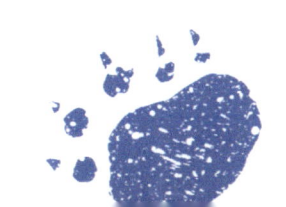

DUSKINGTIDE

somewhere
between
   the last second of day
   first second of night
between
   the daily swap
   of sun and moon

that shadowy veil between
light and dark vanishes in

a wizardly puff

the world is now bewitched
spellbound inside and out

forests are frosted in silver-leafed sleep

fiery red clouds harden into
   black-browed mountains
   clamorous sky creatures

a thousand lost spirits
are set loose in spectral air swirls

bouquets of buried stars
out-pop through purple sky-fields

telltale scents
twine round the low-flying moon

twilight's small sounds
amplify into a chorus of giants

till the deep loud duskingtide
this ancient gloaming
this breathless semi-dark
spins
in one incandescence
into pure night

and with just a
tiny candle-strike

is gone

ALL TANGLED UP

sorry
can't come right now
I'm all tangled up with these words
they're jumping east and
twisting west
itching to be untangled
into a poem

THIS DAY IS TOO BIG

this day is too big
this sky is too grey
this cloud is too fat
my shadow so small

THANK YOU TREE

thank you tree
for all the apples
guess I must have sung
the perfect crunchy spell
last year

152

POOR SNAIL

poor snail
crushed
by some careless foot

what other small
deaths

I wonder

lie hidden in
my garden

LETTER TO THE MOON

dear moon,
once you were so small
so barely breathing
that even the tiniest planets
laughed and danced circles
right over you each evening
and the silver studded comets
ignoring you completely
hurtled past all slapdash glee
towards nowhere special
plus your old friend sun
didn't bother to say a word before
merrily sailing off in some
great blood orange ball

but moon
I have always been here
waiting
every night
so I hope you sleep well
up there

your friend,
me

STOP THE WORLD

stop the world
so I can leap onto
a rainbow and
cartwheel down a
carnival of colour

stop the world
so I can watch
a galaxy of buds as
they unfurl into
starry flowers
slow blink by
slow blink

stop the world
so I can burrow inside
this jagged rock and
explore every ancient and
faraway place
it's ever travelled

stop the world
so I can caper with
the clouds and
float puff-like into
anything I want

stop the world
so I can run roaring
with the lions and
be on their team
whenever they need me

stop the world
so I can smell each
throbbing scent as it
circles and
whirls its way into
the big fat air

stop the world
so I can pop inside
a polka dot
and decorate any
bustling butterfly

stop the world
so I can plunge
under the sea and
discover every
fish-slippery
secret

stop the world
so I can rocket
through the stars
and count all the
zillions of light beams

stop the world
so I can scrunch up in a
soft-sailing snowflake and
see winter through
a prism of shiny crystals

stop the world
so I can look
inside myself and
discover all the

deep-down

ready-to-burst

hidden

magic

157

FLEA'S HAIKU

great jump!

awesome leap!

but if I really try . . .

zoom!

right over the moon!

WHALE'S HAIKU

born all the way in
lost long ago
I deep-dive to . . .

you'll never know

158

RAIN'S HAIKU

oh

the joy of falling

how exhilarating

becoming a

splash

NOISY TOE'S HAIKU

if I wiggle one toe
others join in
can't stop laughing
noisy toes

STORY TIME ORCHESTRA

a story time orchestra
lives inside my book
and when I open
to my favourite part

everyone starts to play

A CONFETTI SKY

when the sun
is finished
each day
it shreds into
a confetti sky
each night

AFTERNOON SHOWERS

colours grow loud
earth grows mud
scents grow long trails
all the way to sunset

MORNING'S HAIKU

morning rolls gentle
into good day
refolds the dark

untwines its light

TWILIGHT'S HAIKU

twilight blur

one by one
stars ignite
as night sky unveils

a slow bloom
moon

PERFECT CRYSTALS HAIKU

everywhere
newborn white flakes
perfect crystals
then gone
perfect riddle

SNOWY OWL'S HAIKU

oh
I sky roll a thousand paths
today

poor earth
can't turn very fast

SNOW'S SONG

I know
I know

hard to be quiet when I arrive
but look
outside is loud with
white puffs
and

not one little sound

SUCH LUCK AGAIN

SNOW
First icy wind of winter.
Such luck!

ICY WIND
First snow of winter.
Such luck!

WINTER
First time I'm appreciated.
Such luck!

LUCK
Told you . . . I'm totally great all year.

WINTER SUN'S HAIKU

guess who!

ice twinkles
snow sparkles
frost gleams

surprised?

it's me!
winter sun

CRUNCHANDSLIDE

when snow falls
everyone rushes to
standinaweandlook
when snow rests
everyone rushes
everywhichway to
crunchandslide then
crunchandslide
againandagainandagainand . . .

PREPOSTEROUS PENGUINS

thousands
of preposterously pensive penguins
pause to participate
in a particularly polar poetry pageant
probably in the perfectly pale and cold
penetrating South Pole
perhaps the precise problem is
every penguin parades around like
a posh peppy peacock
pretentiously presuming
to proclaim in a pesky pernickety way
they should (for pete's sake)
positively peep first

173

TREES AND ME

when night is still day
day still night
I head to the woods
to talk to the trees
I tell them bits and pieces
of this and that
they tell me of last winter
speak of new leaves
and whisper who passes
amongst their roots

twilight

go gently
and let your eye be caught
by little things

ABOUT THE AUTHOR
AND ILLUSTRATOR

Zaro Weil lives on a little farm in southern France. She loves writing and animals and trees and making things up. She has had a lot of fun working with Junli on her fourth children's book, *Cherry Moon*.

(Other Books By Zaro: *Mud, Moon and Me, Firecrackers, Spot Guevara Hero Dog*)

(Zaro's website: zaroweil.com)

Junli Song lives in Chicago in America. She loves colours and patterns and telling stories and printmaking. She has had a wonderful time working on her first book *Cherry Moon* with Zaro.

(Junli's website: www.artsofsong.com)